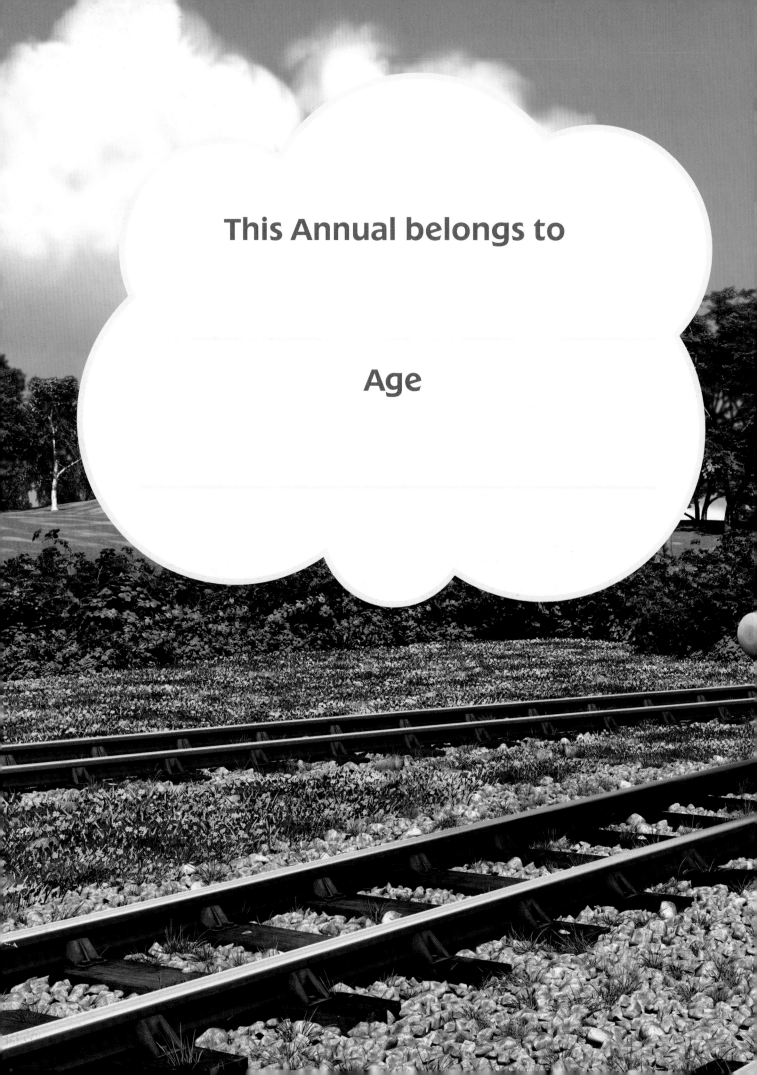

This Annual belongs to

Age

★ Annual 2014 ★

★ Contents ★

EGMONT
We bring stories to life

First published in Great Britain 2013 by Egmont UK Limited
The Yellow Building, 1 Nicholas Road, London W11 4AN
Edited by Laura Green. Designed by Martin Aggett.

Thomas the Tank Engine & Friends™

CREATED BY BRITT ALLCROFT
Based on the Railway Series by the Reverend W Awdry
© 2013 Gullane (Thomas) LLC. A HIT Entertainment company.
Thomas the Tank Engine & Friends and Thomas & Friends are trademarks of Gullane (Thomas) Limited.
Thomas the Tank Engine & Friends and Design is Reg. U.S. Pat. & Tm. Off.

HiT entertainment

ISBN 978 1 4052 6758 8
54717/1
Printed in Italy

A chance to
WIN £150
of book tokens!
See page 67 for details.

NATIONAL
BOOK
tokens

WELCOME TO SODOR!

Welcome to the Thomas Annual! Enjoy the stories and activities, and see if you can be Really Useful too!

★ Meet Thomas ★

Thomas is the Number 1 Engine on Sodor! He always tries his best to be a Really Useful Engine. Everyone loves Thomas – he makes friends wherever he goes!

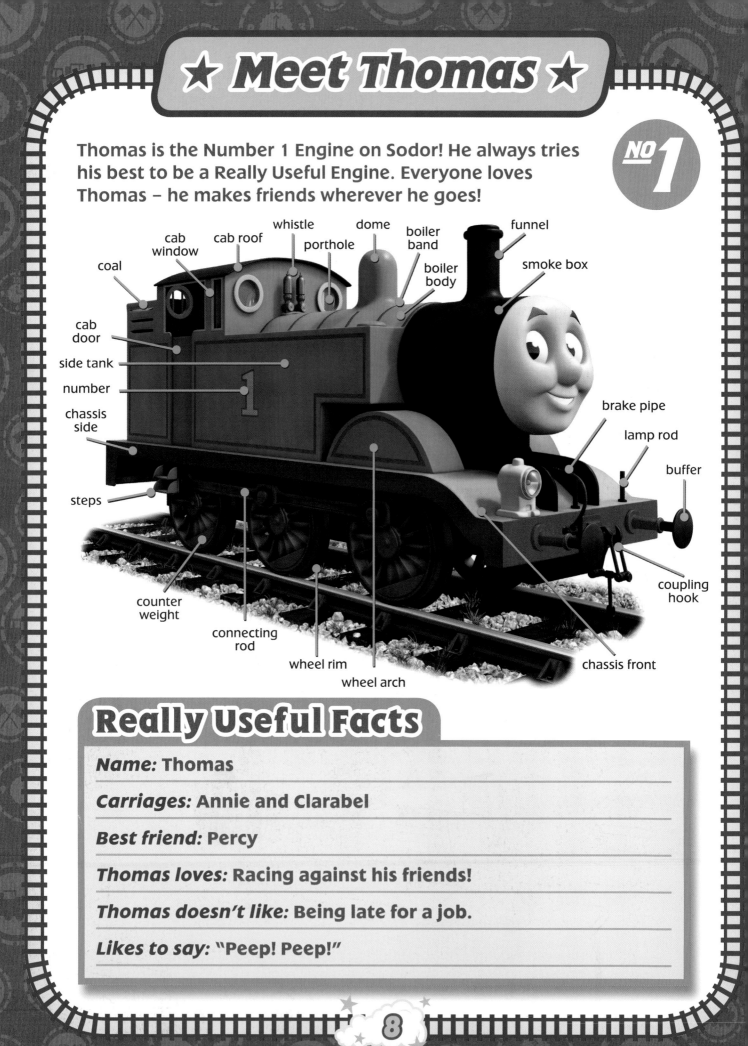

whistle — cab roof — cab window — coal — cab door — side tank — number — chassis side — steps — counter weight — connecting rod — wheel rim — wheel arch — porthole — dome — boiler band — boiler body — funnel — smoke box — brake pipe — lamp rod — buffer — coupling hook — chassis front

Really Useful Facts

Name: Thomas

Carriages: Annie and Clarabel

Best friend: Percy

Thomas loves: Racing against his friends!

Thomas doesn't like: Being late for a job.

Likes to say: "Peep! Peep!"

★ Get Colouring! ★

Use your crayons to colour in this big picture of Thomas.
Trace over his name at the bottom of the page too!

Happy Birthday, Sir!

Today was a special day. It was
The Fat Controller's birthday, and there
was a new car on Sodor. He was called
Winston and he could ride on rails!

"Thomas, take Winston on your jobs today,"
said The Fat Controller. "I'll meet you at
Knapford Station at tea time."

Thomas **beamed** from buffer to buffer.
He was very proud to be helping
The Fat Controller on his birthday!

Salty had a story to tell the engines.

"Many years ago, on his birthday, The Fat Controller visited all the stations on Sodor and had cake with the passengers!"

"Ah, yes, in the oldest carriage on the Island!" said Edward. "Nobody has seen that carriage for years."

"That's nice, Salty," said Thomas. "But we have lots to do. Come on, Winston."

But Winston wasn't thinking about jobs. He was thinking about The Fat Controller's birthday.

The first stop for Thomas and Winston was
Maron Station to pick up some apples.

The workmen coupled up the flatbeds in
no time. Thomas was soon ready to go! But where was
Winston? He wasn't behind Thomas. In fact, Thomas
couldn't see him anywhere.

Suddenly he **burst** out of the bushes!
"Sorry Thomas! I was looking for ..."

But there was no time to listen.
Thomas had too much to do!

The next stop was Farmer Trotter's farm. Farmer Trotter was pleased to see Thomas. The apples were for his pigs – they were getting hungry!

"See how important it is to be on time, Winston?" asked Thomas. But there was no answer.

Winston had disappeared again! But not for long. He soon **whizzed** back onto the track.

"Sorry Thomas! I was looking for …"

But Thomas was already steaming to the next job!

At the Whispering Wood, Winston vanished again.

"Right, you ride in front of me," said Thomas. "Then I can't lose you!"

Suddenly, Winston came to a stop. "Thomas! That's it!"

There, hidden in the bushes, was The Fat Controller's old carriage!

"That's why you kept disappearing," said Thomas. "**Well done**, Winston! Let's give The Fat Controller the best birthday surprise ever!"

At Knapford Station, The Fat Controller was cross. Thomas and Winston were late. Just as he was about to leave, they **raced** into the station.

"**Wait!** We have a surprise for you, Sir!" said Thomas.

Edward **chuffed** up to the platform – pulling the old carriage behind him!

"**Oh my!**" gasped The Fat Controller. "Thank you, Thomas. Thank you, Winston. You have both had a Really Useful day!"

And that made Thomas and Winston happier than ever.

★ Birthday Quiz ★

How much do you remember about the Happy Birthday, Sir! story? Take the quiz to find out!

Tick the boxes when you know the answer. Good luck!

1 Which of these is Winston?

a

b

c

2 What was Winston looking for?

a

MARON

b

c

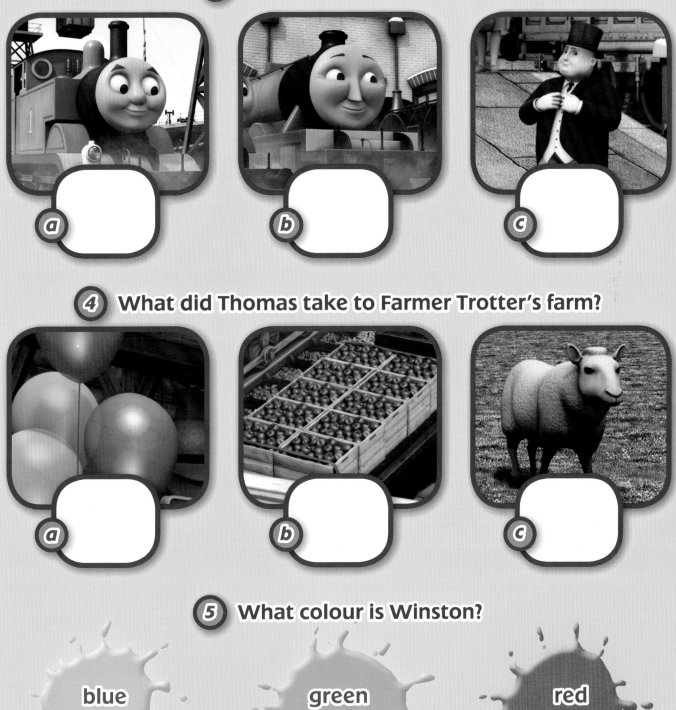

③ Whose birthday was it?

a   *b*   *c*

④ What did Thomas take to Farmer Trotter's farm?

a   *b*   *c*

⑤ What colour is Winston?

blue   green   red

a   *b*   *c*

Answers on page 66.

★ Meet Gordon ★

N⁰ 4

Gordon is the strongest engine in the Steam Team. Gordon likes to pull the Express. But don't ask him to pull heavy goods – that is his worst job!

Really Useful Facts

Name: Gordon

Number: 4

Colour: Blue

Gordon loves: To be the fastest engine on Sodor.

Gordon doesn't like: When other engines beat him in a race!

Likes to say: "Out of the way! Express coming through!"

★ Steam into Trouble ★

Gordon is going too fast and is about to bump into Salty!

Can you spot five differences between these two pictures?

Answers on page 66.

★ Close Call ★

Henry and Charlie are puffing through the snow.

Can you find these close-ups in the big picture?
When you find them, tick the box.

a **b** **c**

★ Jigsaw Jumble ★

Which piece is missing from the jigsaw picture of The Fat Controller and Thomas?

Answers on page 66.

Muddy Matters

Today was the Farmers' Fair. James had two Very Important jobs to do. He was taking Farmer McColl's sheep to the fair and he was having his photograph taken for the newspaper!

"Make sure you take the fast track to the fair. No bumping my sheep about," Farmer McColl had said. "And make sure they stay clean."

"I will keep them as smart as I am, sir!" James said, proudly.

There were two routes to the fair.
One track was fast but muddy. The other track
was bumpy but dry. James didn't want to be dirty
for his photograph, so he took the bumpy track.

The poor sheep **jiggled** about in the back!

"**Bubbling boilers!**" said James. "What a rocky ride!"

The trailer was bumping so hard, the trailer door
flew open!

But James didn't notice. He was too busy
being the cleanest engine on Sodor.

James pulled up next to Emily at Maron Station. He told her about the photograph for the newspaper. He was so busy showing off, he didn't hear the clack of the trailer. Or the **clatter** of little hooves …

The sheep had escaped!

"**Fenders and fireboxes!**" said James, when he saw a sheep on the platform. "Come back!"

But it was too late. The sheep escaped to the bottom of the field.

The fast train track to the sheep was muddy.
So James took the dry track instead. He couldn't
get dirty before his photograph!

But the track was very long. By the time James found the
sheep, they had already moved away.

"Bother!" said James. Then he had an idea. Katy the
sheepdog could round up the sheep. Katy barked and
sure enough the sheep trotted over to James.

"It's working!" said James. "All I have to
do is wait here and stay clean!"

James was so excited he let out a whistle. **TOOT!** But the sheep got such a surprise, they ran back into the field and through a muddy puddle!

"Oh no! We can't be late!" cried James. "It doesn't matter if I'm dirty. I can't let Farmer McColl down."

So James **whooshed** like the wind down the fast, dirty track. Soon, James wasn't a bright, red engine. He was a muddy, messy one!

James pulled up next to the sheep and Katy pushed them into the trailer. They were back on track!

When James pulled up at the fair Farmer McColl gasped. Not only was James covered in mud but so were his sheep!

"**Splendid!**" said the newspaper photographer. "A hard-working engine with his sheep, straight from the fields. That's a front-page photograph! Smile, everyone!"

James **beamed** from buffer to buffer. He had never been happier to be the dirtiest engine on Sodor!

★ Counting Sheep ★

How many sheep can you count?
Write the number in the box.

I can count [　　] sheep.

Answers on page 66.

★ Special Deliveries ★

Thomas and his friends all have special deliveries to make today. Follow the wiggly tracks to find out what they are delivering.

1 Thomas

2 Percy

3 Charlie

a fish

b apples

c milk churns

Answers on page 66.

★ Meet Percy ★

Percy is a small engine who is full of fun! He is Thomas' best friend and he pulls the mail train. He has lots of accidents too – like crashing into a truck of treacle!

PERCY NO 6
No. 6 Green Engine

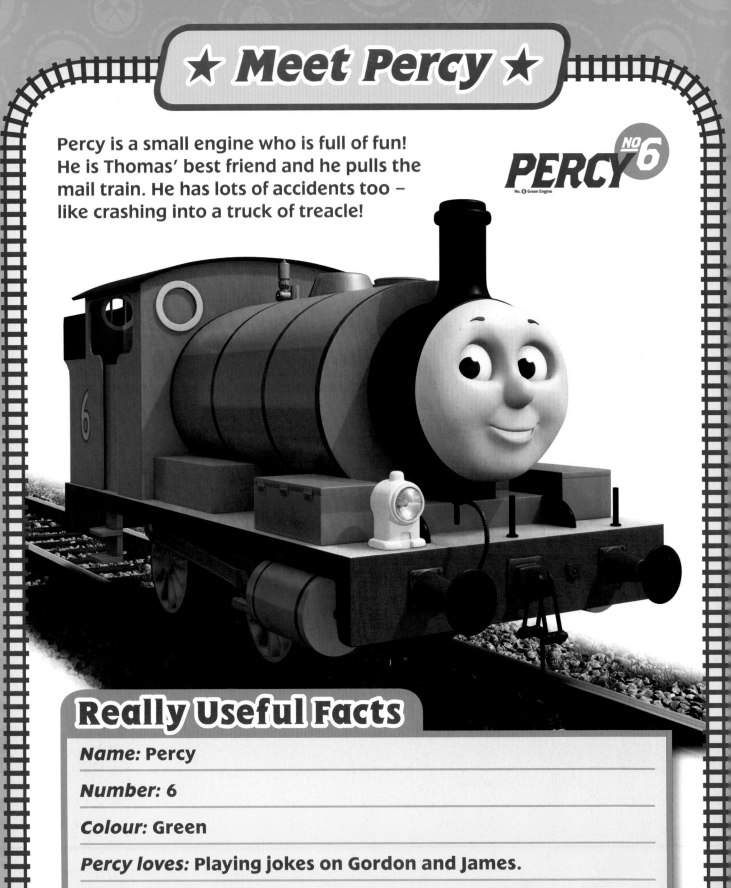

Really Useful Facts

Name: Percy

Number: 6

Colour: Green

Percy loves: Playing jokes on Gordon and James.

Percy doesn't like: Being called a green caterpillar!

Likes to say: "Mail coming through!"

★ Birthday Time! ★

It's Thomas' birthday! Percy wants to make him a birthday card.

Can you help by drawing a nice picture on the card? You could draw a picture of Percy, some balloons or a birthday cake!

Happy Birthday!

There's a party at Knapford Station!

These pictures look the same, but there are 5 differences in picture 2.

Colour a balloon for each difference you find.

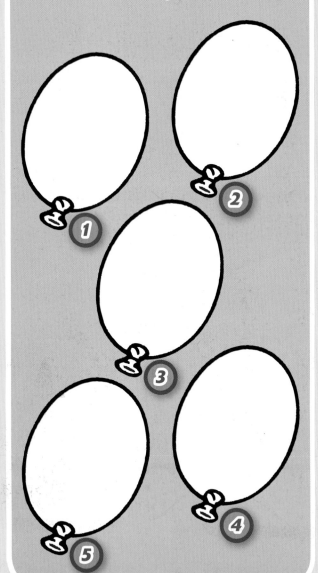

1

2

3

5

4

1

2

Answers on page 66.

★ Meet James ★

James is a very proud engine. He takes tiptop care of his red paintwork. He can sometimes get into trouble for showing off though!

JAMES NO5

No. 5 Red Engine

Really Useful Facts

Name: James

Number: 5

Colour: Red

James loves: Pulling the Express when Gordon is away.

James doesn't like: Getting dirty!

Likes to say: "I am a Splendid Engine!"

★ Pink Picture ★

Oh no! James has been painted pink by mistake!
He's not very happy.

Can you find the **four** objects at the bottom of the page
in the big picture? Tick a box when you spot one.

a

b

c

d

Answers on page 66.

★ Odd One Out ★

Which of these Sodor friends is the odd one out?

THOMAS

HIRO

BERTIE

GORDON

Answer on page 66.

★ Shadow Match ★

Draw lines to match Thomas and his friends
to their shadows.

Answers on page 66.

Hiro is special engine. He is very old and was forgotten for many years ... until Thomas found him again! Now he is a very happy engine!

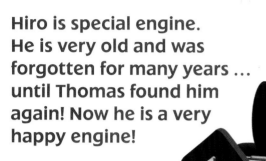

MASTER of the **RAILWAY**
The Island Of Sodor

Really Useful Facts

Name: Hiro

Colour: Black and gold

History: Hiro is from Japan.

Fun fact: Hiro's friends call him "The Master of the Railway"!

Hiro loves: Pulling flower trucks.

Hiro doesn't like: Missing home in Japan.

★ My Home ★

Hiro loves to talk about his home in Japan. Now he wants to find out where you live!

Can you draw a picture of your home? Remember to draw the doors and windows and anything else you want to show Hiro.

★ Station Spot ★

Can you help The Fat Controller find these 5 things at Knapford Station?

1. Family

2. Luggage

40

Tick the boxes as you find them!

3. Lampost

4. Cleaner

5. Wall Clock

41

You can help read this story. Join in when you see the picture.

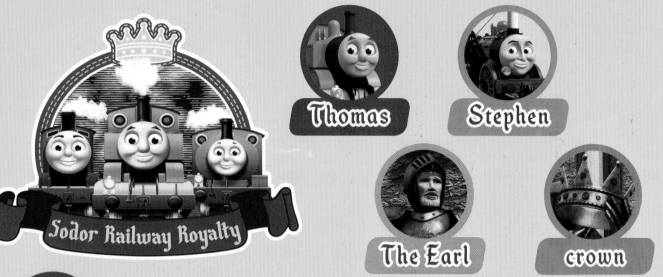

Sodor Railway Royalty

Thomas

Stephen

The Earl

crown

 and his friends were very excited.

Something special was happening on Sodor.

 was rebuilding the old castle! Percy, James and needed to work as a team to help him. "Sir, why are we fixing the castle?" said . "It's a big surprise," said .

 had brought his old engine  but

he had to be repaired first. Victor fixed his

funnel and boiler and gave him a new coat of

paint. "Now you look Really Useful again!"

said  .

 wished he could be useful again but didn't know how. "You can be," said. "  has a top secret job for you!"  steamed off to get started. But he got trapped in an old mine where he found a gold  !

 worked hard to rescue his friend from the mine.  was very happy.  had found the gold  ! It had been missing for years. "Your special job is to show visitors around the castle!" peeped  .  would be a Really Useful Engine again!

King of the Railway!

★ Meet Stephen ★

Stephen is one of the oldest steam engines on Sodor. Although he isn't very fast now, he used to be known as The Rocket years ago!

The Rocket

Really Useful Facts

Name: Stephen

Nickname: The Rocket

Colour: Yellow and black

Stephen loves: Helping out at the castle.

Stephen doesn't like: Being left out.

Likes to say: "How can I help?"

★ Design a Badge ★

Many years ago, Stephen was given a badge.
Now you can make him a new badge!

Grab your brightest crayons and design a badge
below – you could draw a picture of Stephen,
a castle or anything else you can think of!

Stephen
The Rocket

★ Mine Maze ★

Help Thomas find a path through the maze to rescue Stephen from the old mine.

START

FINISH

★ Meet Spencer ★

Spencer is a super-fast silver engine who likes to show off. He always thinks he is right, even when he's wrong!

Really Useful Facts

Name: *Spencer*

Colour: *Silver*

Fun fact: *He takes the Duke and Duchess of Boxford around Sodor when they visit!*

Spencer doesn't like: *When engines are faster than him!*

Most likely to say: *"Look how fast I am, everyone!"*

★ Time to Steam ★

START

Spencer is about to race! You can join in too.

Set a stopclock to see how long it takes you to race your finger along the track. Count up the flags along the way!

FINISH

Answers on page 66.

Toot toot!

Thomas coming through!

Follow the instructions to make your very own Thomas the Tank Engine costume.

You will need:

★ A3 piece of black card

★ 2 disposable bowls, painted black

★ Glue (or double-sided sticky tape)

★ Ribbon

★ An old pillowcase (preferably blue)

★ Scissors

★ Coloured paper

★ A paper plate

To make the hat:

1 Roll up the piece of card into a funnel shape and secure with tape.

2 Glue the two painted bowls together, rim to rim.

3 Tape the bowls onto the tube.

4 Secure around your head with a ribbon.

Costume ★

To make the outfit:

1 Cut slits for the head and arms in the top and sides of the pillowcase.

2 Cut out the number 1 from yellow paper.

3 Stick it onto red paper and cut out again, leaving a border of red around the yellow number.

4 Glue or tape the number to the pillowcase.

Glue

5 Draw a simple Thomas face onto the plate. Cut out holes for the eyes and secure around the head with ribbon.

Peep, peep and off you go!

★ 1 2 3 ... GO! ★

Thomas and Diesel are having a race to see who's faster – Steamies or Diesels!

Choose who'll be Thomas and who'll be Diesel, then get ready to race to the Finish!

START

FINISH

21
You crash! Move backwards 1 space.

20

19

How to Play:

You can play this game with a friend. You will need a dice, and a counter each. The first person to roll a 6 starts. Take turns to roll the dice and move your counters. The first person across the finish line wins!

18
The turntable gets you in a spin! Throw a 3 to move on.

17

16
You get stuck in a mine. Go back 2 spaces.

15

1

2

3 You stop at a red flag. Go back to the start.

4

5 A truck bumps you forwards 2 spaces.

6

7

8

9 Water floods the track. Go back 3 spaces.

14

13 You are fast! Move forwards 2 spaces.

12

11

10

★ Meet Emily ★

Emily is painted emerald green – she really stands out! She can be bossy but she will always help her friends. She's like a big sister to some of the engines.

EXCELLENT EMILY!

Really Useful Facts

Name: *Emily*

Colour: *Emerald green*

Pulls: *Passenger coaches*

Emily loves: *Being right!*

Emily doesn't like: *When the engines won't do as she says.*

Most likely to say: *"Don't call me Little Miss Bossy Buffers!"*

★ Excellent Emily ★

Emily has brought lots of passengers to the fair.
What a Useful Engine!

Can you find the close-ups in the big picture?
When you find them, tick the box and say 'Excellent Emily!'

a

b

c

d

Emily's Winter Party

It was winter on the Island of Sodor. The wind **whistled** and **wheeshed** through the engines' wheels. But that didn't stop the engines smiling, because it was a very special day. It was the Winter Festival that night.

"The most helpful engine will be this year's Party Engine and pull the present train," said The Fat Controller.

Emily crept forward eagerly. But The Fat Controller gave jobs to Thomas and Henry and asked Emily to wait.

Just then, a big gust of wind **whipped** The Fat Controller's hat from his head!

"**My hat!**" said The Fat Controller. "Oh dear. I can't go to the party without my hat."

Suddenly, an idea flew into Emily's funnel.

"Please Sir, I will find your hat," said Emily.

"Thank you, Emily! That would be very helpful indeed!" said The Fat Controller.

Emily was excited. Maybe she would pull the present train after all.

Emily **clickety-clacked** along the track.
But she forgot to look for The Fat Controller's hat.
She was too excited about being the Party Engine.

Emily met Thomas at a crossing where some
children were building a snowman nearby.

"Hello, Thomas. The Fat Controller has lost his hat.
I'm going to find it and be the Party Engine," she said.

Emily's firebox **fizzed** with joy!

Soon, Emily reached the Steamworks and an idea **popped** into her pistons.

"I'll collect the present train now!" she thought.

So Emily was coupled to the present train and decorated with lights. But then The Fat Controller arrived. He was very cross.

"I'm sorry, Sir. I forgot to find your hat. I don't deserve to be the Party Engine," said Emily.

Thomas had been working hard, so he was decorated as the Party Engine instead.

Thomas **puffed** through the night pulling the present train. But Emily didn't notice. She was thinking about The Fat Controller's hat.

Thomas and Emily stopped at the crossing where the children had built their snowman. The lights from the present train lit up the field.

"Thomas! **Look!**" cried Emily.

And there, by the side of the tracks, was The Fat Controller's hat - on the snowman's head! Emily was so pleased!

At the Winter Festival, the children were having a wonderful time. But The Fat Controller wasn't happy without his hat.

Then Thomas and Emily **wheeshed** into the station.

"Please Sir, I have a present for you," said Emily.

The guard gave The Fat Controller his top hat!

"Thank you!" he cried. "You are a very helpful engine."

Emily felt so proud, she thought her boiler might **burst!**

★ My Present ★

Thomas has brought a present for you too!
Is it a toy, a pet or something different?
Draw a picture of your
present in the box.

☆ Thomas Song ☆

Thomas he's the cheeky one,
James is vain but lots of fun.
Percy pulls the mail on time,
Gordon thunders down the line.
Emily really knows her stuff,
Henry toots and huffs and puffs,
Edward wants to help and share,
Toby, well let's say, he's square!

They're 2, they're 4, they're 6, they're 8,
Shunting trucks and hauling freight.
Red and green and brown and blue,
They're the Really Useful crew!

All with different roles to play
Round Tidmouth Sheds or far away.
Down the hills and round the bends,
Thomas and his friends!

Goodbye!

THOMAS 1

PERCY 6

EMILY

EDWARD 2

JAMES 5

GORDON 4

HENRY 3

TOBY 7

Page 16-17:
1 - b, 2 - a, 3 - c, 4 - b, 5 - c.

Page 19: ▼

Page 21:
Jigaw piece b is missing from the puzzle.

Page 28:
There are 8 sheep.

Page 29:
1 - c, 2 - a, 3 - b.

Page 32-33: ▼

Page 36: Bertie is the odd one out because he is a bus. The other friends are engines.

Page 37: 1 - c, 2 - d, 3 - a, 4 - b.

Page 40-41: ▼

Page 48-49: ▼

Page 51:
The are 7 green flags.

Thomas Reader Survey 2014

We'd love to know what you think about your Thomas Annual.

Ask a grown-up to help you fill in this form and post it to the address at the end by 28th February 2014, or you can fill in the survey online at: www.egmont.co.uk/thomas-survey2014

One lucky reader will win £150 of book tokens. Five runners up will win a £25 book token each.

1. Who bought this annual?

☐ Me

☐ Parent/guardian

☐ Grandparent

☐ Other (please specify)

....

2. Why did they buy it?

☐ Christmas present

☐ Birthday present

☐ I'm a collector

☐ Other (please specify)

....

3. What are your favourite parts of the annual?

Stories	☐ Really like	☐ Like	☐ Don't like
Puzzles	☐ Really like	☐ Like	☐ Don't like
Colouring	☐ Really like	☐ Like	☐ Don't like
Meet the Engine pages	☐ Really like	☐ Like	☐ Don't like
Songs and rhymes	☐ Really like	☐ Like	☐ Don't like
Things to make	☐ Really like	☐ Like	☐ Don't like

4. Do you think the stories are too long, too short or about right?

☐ Too long ☐ Too short ☐ About right

5. Do you think the activities are too hard, too easy or about right?

☐ Too hard ☐ Too easy ☐ About right

6. Apart from Thomas, who are your favourite characters?

1. ....
2. ....
3. ....

7. Which other annuals do you like?

1. ....
2. ....
3. ....

8. What is your favourite …

1. … app or website? ....
2. … console game? ....
3. … magazine? ....
4. … book? ....

9. What are your favourite TV programmes?

1. ....
2. ....
3. ....

10. Would you like to get the Thomas Annual again next year?

☐ Yes   ☐ No

Why? ....

....

Name: .... Age: .... Boy ☐ Girl ☐

Signature: ....

Email address: ....

Daytime telephone number: ....

☐ Please send me the Egmont Monthly Catch-Up Newsletter.

Please cut out and post to:

Thomas Annual Reader Survey, Egmont UK Limited,

The Yellow Building, 1 Nicholas Road, London, W11 4AN   *Good luck!*

ADVERTISEMENT
THOMAS & FRIENDS™
LOOK OUT FOR THOMAS & FRIENDS MAGAZINES!
ALPHABET SPECIAL
THOMAS & FRIENDS
THOMAS EXPRESS
Issue No. 325
EXTRA COLOURING PAGES
INSIDE CHALKBOARD STICKERS CRAYONS
It's as easy as ABC!
Look! Great FREE gifts!
30 THOMAS ALPHABET PUZZLES TO KEEP YOU BUSY, PLUS GAMES + STORIES TOO!
ON SALE EVERY 4 WEEKS!
FREE 6 PIECE PLAY SET!
Help me to run the railways!
GORDON'S FACT FILE All you need to know!
THOMAS & FRIENDS
I'll make it through the snow!
MORE STORIES TO READ!
ON SALE EVERY 3 WEEKS!
FREE GIFT WITH EVERY ISSUE!
Thomas and his friends bring you the best puzzles and stories, colouring and fun things to do! Don't miss these two great magazines!
EGMONT
© 2013 Gullane (Thomas) Ltd.